ALEJANDRO CUEVAS-SOSA

Yauh

THE INNER EXIT

0

Grosvenor House
Publishing Limited

All rights reserved
Yauh
The inner exit

© Copyright to the author, Spanish version 1988-9, English version 2007, 2018

The right of Andres Alejandro Cuevas-Sosa to be identified as
the author of this work has been asserted in accordance with Section 78
of the Copyright, Designs and Patents Act 1988 of the United Kingdom

© Copyright of 10/3/2014 to the author for the picture (a caterpillar)
of front cover, back cover and spine background

This book is published by
Grosvenor House Publishing Ltd
Link House
140 The Broadway, Tolworth, Surrey, KT6 7HT.
www.grosvenorhousepublishing.co.uk

This book is sold subject to the conditions that it shall not, by way of
trade or otherwise, be lent, resold, hired out or otherwise circulated
without the author's or publisher's prior consent in any form of binding or
cover other than that in which it is published and
without a similar condition including this condition being imposed
on the subsequent purchaser.

Translated from Spanish into English by a teamwork formed
by Thelma Tangassi Aparicio and the author, of course, the completed work is
author's
full responsibility.

No part of this book may be reproduced in any form, by photocopying or by
any electronic or mechanical means, including information storage or
retrieval systems, without permission in writing from the copyright owner.

A CIP record for this book
is available from the British Library

ISBN 978-1-78623-286-1

To Jacaranda Luna, with eternal love

CONTENTS

Chapter 1 1

Chapter 2 4

Chapter 3 7

Chapter 4 9

Chapter 5 12

Chapter 6 14

Chapter 7 16

Chapter 8 18

Chapter 9 21

Chapter 10 24

Chapter 11 26

Chapter 12 28

Chapter 13 30

Chapter 14 32

Chapter 15 35

Chapter 16 38

Chapter 17 43

Chapter 18 46

1

I did not understand if my dazzled eyes had lost the sight or they did not know how to see what was happening. Hesitant, I clung to the routine life from which I was fleeing and with the absurd intention of returning, I clumsy walked by where I believed was the road of return. It was in this way as I discovered that from the movement of my body beams of light emanated. My movements produced brightness. Thus, I needed to retreat or to go on, fleeing. It was not possible to stay immobile at that dark place to which I was pushed by the uncertainty of my existence. I could not avoid it. The more efforts I made to return I imagined myself more inside.

Just because of not feeling defeated again and aided by my scarce light, I tried to know where that tunnel would carry me off. At night, I arrived at its inner exit, and starting from that moment, I felt the strange sensation that I could be that which surrounded me and, at the same time, be myself. Dazed, I believed to be approaching to the infinite, as if I were, in fact, the infinite. Moreover, even more disturbing it was to suppose, then, that the infinite, more than distance or time, it is option, it is whole, it is all.

When I succeeded in leaving the tunnel, I found the birth of two roads. One of them seemed clear and easy to walk, while the other one, after a short distance, looked hidden and sinking behind a rock. Through this sidewalk, the twinkling of a greenish yellow radiance attracted me. When I surpassed the rock, an iridescent waterfall emerged in front of me. I ran until I arrived to the well formed in the base of the cascade, to get soaked from its luminous water. Because of the unlike breeze which sprinkled, I noticed that the liquid fall was not uniform, but rather infinity of isolated drops hastened to the void; they were cluster-shaped drops and clusters of multi-coloured drops.

I continued recognizing the surroundings and I perceived that the bell-shaped of the flowers of an aretillo transmitted certain nostalgia. Besides, the drops that grazed my lips had a moderate salted flavour and those that touched my skin made me cry. On high, crashing with the clouds, the radiance framed the moment in which the torrent came off from the earth: the waterfall flew. I wanted to climb but could not see how to arrive to such heights. All that I reached to glimpse was the silhouette of a leafy jacaranda. Their roots surged mighty, sticking to the rock and trapping it firmly while the ends sank in the little lagoon. Upon submerging, I began to feel a sudden and inevitable change: my body softened, until it became water. Yes, I ended up turning into a cluster, an insignificant cluster and, even worse, I caught its essence of salty sadness. I allowed myself to be sucked by the root and so I went up by its sap until I sprouted, in the branches of the crown, in the form of nectar of their purplish flowers. I felt as flying: the joyfulness of the jacaranda had invaded me. Not only did I lose the control of my body, but also the one of my mood.

Confused in those branches I discovered where the crown of light that enlightened the waterfall was coming from. Hundreds, thousands of millions of trembling fireflies gave origin to a spring of luminous water. Every time they emitted their hesitant light, from their eyes sprouted tears like lanterns and they were those that formed the water in clusters. The wisest fireflies, in order to counteract their sadness, approached to suck from the flowers of the jacaranda, which allowed me to speak to them.

— What world did my search bring me to?
— Which search? —they asked.

… I could only remember that the sensation that there is a point through which it is possible to penetrate and discover the most hiding of our secrets overwhelmed me. That my spirit poked, pore to pore, in all the corners of my body, until, without knowing what I did, I remained in the dark, I could not retain me and I escaped of myself. As if, I had fallen in a trap.

— But what place is this?
— The spaces of light —they said.
— Are these the spaces of light?
— Yes, these are.
— Where does this road take you?
— It leads to the space of origins.
— Does it lead to the space of origins? What is that?
— By any chance, do you know what your origin is?
— …
— If you are interested, here you can find that answer and perhaps others more.
— I would rather know why you are crying. I would not like to finish the same way you are.

By their silence, they reflected the doubt of whether they would tell me their story. Finally, they decided to do it. "We come from the firmament —they said—. The stars, fireflies of the Universe, are our mothers; that is why we share the twinkling of our light".

But, why you are not with them? —I asked. "One time the youth of the Earth captured us, we got too close and because of the attraction of this planet it was impossible for us to return. Soon it began to rain and, from then on, the rain makes us sad because we understand that they are crying. You will have noticed that when it rains the rivers and the cascades, the lakes and the sea turn stormy, disturbed by the eternal pain of the stars that have lost their daughters, the fireflies".

> — It seems that there is no joyfulness inside you.
> — If the nostalgia controls us, we will be at risk of remaining without light, that is why the jacarandas help us, but since they blossom only in the wintertime one should store nectar so that our longing for living lasts all year. We are victims, the same as you, from the close relationship that there is between the temptations and the freedom.

It was like a punishment. If going on meant to continue like a weak clustery drop and this way getting deeper in the most intimate part of that which surrounded me, I would rather not do it.

It was dawning. The first rays of the Sun, aggressive, reached me soon. I became transformed in vapour of water, invisible vapour that floated inattentive.

2

Although I had preferred to travel without a specific direction, it startled me that in the distance, the clouds got concentrated and I was thrown towards them by the wind. I felt, upon integrating me to its shaken vapours, an urgent call. It was about the implacable attraction that on the water the sterile sands exercise and the chronic thirst of the plants and of the animals of the desert: I was at imminent risk of being consumed by the dryness.

The clouds got crowded fearfully and upon crashing, caused aggressive lightning, preparing in this way the torrential precipitation that was coming. Mixed with the sound of the wind, like a warning, another hoarse and broken whistle was distinguished. Suddenly, without resisting to that call and when the density of the heap was so that we could stand neither the wait nor our turbulent vicinity, millions of clusters of drops rushed to the void. Thus, avoiding hurling myself through canyons and cliffs, I was confronted with the avidity of the sand dunes. For moments, I remained caught in the grottos, later, I felt myself confused in the agitation of rivers, lagoons and ephemeral wells. That way we alleviated, even for a short while, an urgent necessity.

During my uneven walk, I always heard, competing with the pounding of the storm, a hiss. As soon as I could, I tried to locate its origin, without succeeding. Just when I reached it, it remained quiet, to continue going farther away. Therefore, more and more, it took me towards the interior of the desert, until I felt its prisoner, at the mercy of its silent inhabitants.

When the storm was over, just silence remained, and I took refuge in the water that rested in a nest of yellowish and rough rock, an oscillating shade also protected me. Without expecting it, hidden in the silence the hiss exploded deafening: they were cicadas that produced it. With caution, I approached to the rickety shrub of oregano that offered its timid shade, in which they rested.

— Why do you live here? —I asked.
— It is because we are the sentries of the desert.
— To what is it due the insistence of your singing?
— It is necessary in order to alert all who inhabit the stuffy silence.
— But what happened here? Why is so much mystery due?

> — Nobody no longer remembers —they said with soft voice, in contrast with their strident singing— that there was a time in which the Sun used to send solid rays; crystallized firebrands that made impossible to distinguish night from day.

My presence not only made reappeared the signal in order to soothe the aridity of the desert, but it also incited its thirsty inhabitants. Because of its harassing, I began evaporating.

> — And how did the rest of beings of the Earth respond? —I asked them pretending serenity.
> — They protested upon realizing they were invaded by the rain of solid rays, throwing them away of their territory. The rays in vain explained that their intention was not to bother, for that, they had to leave moving towards places less inhabitable and with a more extreme climate, until remaining confined in the deserts.
> — How inhospitable territory they left to them.
> — Resigned, they had to accept that they would never leave those regions. That is why the desert is a reserve, a reserve for undesirable beings. From that time on, the suns decided to deprive its rays of the solidity that was conform them and throw its essence all over the places.

Without being able to postpone more the calling of the dryness, the vapours again, in the shape of whirls of infuriated clouds, we rained on others or maybe on the same places in the desert. Later I became vapour again. I heard the hiss and located its origin; now they rested on a bisnaga. Under its protection, we continued our chat.

> — And how did your drama finish?
> — The solid rays, modelled by the wind, started acquiring vegetable characteristics and from there appeared the most solitary and defensive plants out of all the known ones: the cactuses. When it rains, eyes of shiny colours sprout, with lashes in the shape of petals. With them, they make sure that after the rain, the desert remains at rest. You must have seen them covered with thorns, always willing to refuse any aggression. In addition, through them, they keep informed about the climate changes.
> — And what destiny did the crystallized firebrands that fell in the sea have?
> — At the coast, they formed the coral reef. The proud cactuses of the desert are brothers of blood of the sea coral, which seem gentle but they also live on the defensive.

From the moment we spoke about the denial that the cactuses suffered, the wind became more intense; I could not maintain myself in the bisnaga so I was dragged until I remained stuck on the fleshy columns of an old saguaro. Once again, I found the cicadas; it was always three identical and I never knew who spoke, whether it was the three of them who did it or if the warm echo of the desert multiplied their voice and, maybe, even their image.

> — I think I understand why you love the cactuses.
> — When the dryness is about to explode in uncontrollable fire, they emit a hoarse and broken sound that attracts the clouds so that they can join over the desert and let fall their clusters of drops. We call this sign the voice of the cactuses, and there is no way that clouds avoid to hear it.

The desert remained immobile and the wind insisted in my leaving. The cicadas emitted their monotonous chant until the night fell, but now it sounded to me like an endless lament. The cold took the night and it disguised it of a threatening silence. We are protected, I thought, trying to calm down, by plants that transcended times of chaos.

3

In spite of the cold night, I had conserved myself as vapour of water and, upon dawning, a tall and strong man, and a huitzil of magenta tail were in front of me. I distracted contemplating their presence: The first one carried with dignity a lance of ebony, with an ivory point, while the bird displayed, like a thorn, its hooked beak. When both of them were prepared to calm their thirst, inadvertently they aspirated me and I passed to form part of their nature. Within them, without saying a word, we conversed from thought to thought and I watched the images that came to their mind.

> — I would like to stop being water —I asked them, being sorry about my distraction.
> — We do not know how to help you, we have some problems to solve —they answered—. We hope that you are not a load for us.

In spite of them and of myself, in their being I felt guarded again. I realized that the desert hid their escape. The man, named Tao, avoided the dangers, while the huitzil chose the direction less risky. Tao was an afflicted warrior who as an adolescent had to kill a wild bull, sacred animal that attacked him unexpectedly. His tribe interpreted it as a bad presage. As a punishment, they threatened to sacrifice him, and he got sick of terror. He had to flee and hire himself as a servant for a foreign family, but his increasing desperation obliged him to continue fleeing. From that experience, all of a sudden he was invaded by images of furious horned. One of them, to whom the rest followed, was the most furious and dangerous; he had killed this one.

Disturbed because of the bellows, the man suffered of fright, especially at night, when the harassment of the bull was constant. At various occasions, hidden in the darkness, the animal was about to take revenge. Its flaming eyes erased the shades. Its snort cracked and dissolved the clouds, and the paws hurt with scorn the ground leaving wells like traps.

The morning when I was aspired, after wandering until the night fell, Tao was very alarmed since the wild animal penned him without the possibility of escaping. Finally, he no longer could avoid the confronting and two dark masses that at close turned red started a conflict of thrusting and crashes.

The gladiator, challenging, waved his lance with the ivory-like sharp end to the hot red and set fire to the night with the traces that followed his quick and threatening movements. Tao knew that you could only defeat the wild bulls if you succeed in turning off their eyes, since when they are left blind they flee until extinguishing. In one of the attacks, the monster hit the weapon with its horns and broke it. The gigantic warrior kept a piece of lance in each hand and tried to destroy the eyes of the beast, but its horns, like lightning, with the least movement removed any threat. Fiercely they rolled by the dunes fighting body to body and at times it looked like two balls of fire were united, as if the bull, as a matter of fact, were part of Tao; and I, inside him, without knowing how to escape.

At last, the fight ceased and the almost dying image of the bull was lost giving tumbles in a disorderly race. The gladiator lay lifeless and, leaning on his left shoulder, Huitzil accompanied him, pendent of that man's heartbeats and breath. From its curved beak drops of blood dripped.

— I want to stop fleeing —Tao stammered, still frightened.
— Our spirit, in order to survive, imposes us to be free —Huitzil said.

In the distance, the mild turbulence that the cascades make was listened. The fight made me feel how much life enslaves. In contrast, the unrestrained Universe looked at us, showing us the multitude of lights that placed at random, result from the disorder that is born from the absolute freedom; freedom inherent to inert matter, truly free, authentically it, genuinely light.

The foliage of thistles covered us. An undecided moon in the last quarter of the moon accompanied us and, finally, we listened to the murmur of the water again.

4

Time went away, since upon waking up we had, in the horizon, a flaming sun about to rest or maybe the rise of a bright full moon that was about to fly towards the heights of the night. I was worried about how to escape from Tao's and from Huitzil's nature, I wanted to return to be myself and stop mixing my wishes with the ones of them.

Soon it got dark. With the watchful moon, the twinkling of a yellow-greenish radiance competed. We were attracted to it; I supposed that we were going to the abounding place of the waterfall, but the wind opposed every time more intense. Actually, when we succeeded in arriving we sheltered leaned on the back of a castor-oil plant that originated just at the beginning of the waterfall, and we were astonished to discover that the millions of fireflies had interrupted their nostalgic rest and they shook their wings with exaltation. We noticed that their movement was synchronic and it followed a growing and sustained rhythm, broken by a brief interval in which it was attenuated, in order to take impulse again and repeat the sequence. Upon intensifying the fluttering, the fireflies made blasts that raised the radiant cascade, generating the waving sway of currents that went up and down; winding line of water in fragments.

Suddenly, the beat of their wings became so intense that the blast threw toward the bottom of the night an immense torrent that swallowed us. Tao and Huitzil felt their body hurt and dazed, and they were breathing with difficulty. Prisoners in the torrent, we were obliged to endure the panic of an uncertain journey.

An infinity number of hexagonal cells upholstered the spherical place that contained us. Inside them, a disturbing activity was appreciated and through their crystalline bottom, the exterior was seen. Tao and Huitzil, fearful, remained one next to the other on the alveolar wall. Their breathing ended up by getting adapted.

Without realizing, leaning on his walking stick, an old man of wavy beard and hair appeared. His eyes, colour of light, watched with special intensity. The fear and astonishment that the faces of Tao and Huitzil reflected must have been a lot, since he tried to calm them down with a smile and, besides, he offered them royal jelly that he was eating.

— Where are you taking us? —Tao asked him with anxiety.
— To sow universal life —the gentle old man answered.
— To sow universal life, what are you talking about? —Huitzil asked.
— First of all, tell us who you are. What is your name? —Tao interrupted.
— My name is Cometa.
— What do you mean by sowing universal life? —Huitzil insisted.
— You have just witnessed what a few have seen: the birth of a comet —he answered—. The virtuous beat of wings is called, in the spaces of light, the dance of the fireflies, and it obeys to valuable aims of universal repercussions. On earth, the dance of the fireflies, sustained and intense, serves to give impulse to the rivers and takes them through all its corners; otherwise, they would stop and only would form lakes. The rivers, upon watering the valleys met when passing by, spread, generous, thousands of tears in cluster, where beings of all kinds originate. However, when the flutter increases their impulse, they throw through the air the column of the waterfall and project it toward the space, with the strength of an eruption, spreading in this way their luminous load of embryos and seeds. The comets are, as you can see now, sowers of life and matter that wander throughout the Universe.

During the journey, portions of the comet were detaching, like blazes. I had wanted no longer be part of Tao and of Huitzil's nature, but it was more certain not to be exposed.

— Are they sowers of life and matter? —Tao asked.
— Yes, live and inert matter shares the same origin, the tears of the fireflies, and the same essence, the light of those clustered drops. From there that everything is the same, but different.
— And on earth, what is it born from them? —Huitzil asked.
— If it is a tear that sprouted by day, for its contact with the Sun it will give origin to a plant; but if it came off at night, to one of so many animals, from there that the Moon produces them many worries. There also are unanimated species that arose by day, as the amber, and others that belong to the night, as the star sapphire. It occur the same with numerous stony forms that, in their look, reflect their origin. As you can understand, life is presence and all that exists belong to it. That is the universal life.
— If everything surges from the clusters of tears, then do the inert also suffer? —Tao asked.
— That is right. The suffering is a perennial companion of the different forms of universal life.

"I know it from my own experience", I had wanted to tell Cometa, when unexpectedly he spoke to me:

— Why do you hide, Yauh, if you have some questions to make?

Feeling myself uncovered precipitated that, through the tears of Tao and Huitzil, I was separated from their being. I fused my watery halves and, helped by the generating ambience of life of the comet, I recovered the human form and its characteristic opacity. The sudden apparition of the old man helped so that my presence did not alarm them and, on the contrary, they showed curiosity for meeting me.

— Ask, then, without hesitations —Cometa insisted.
— Why was I transformed in water? —I claimed him.
— It was necessary that you shared your essence with the unanimated forms, to which you have not allowed yourself to appreciate. Besides, you wanted to get on the jacaranda; you fulfilled your wish.
— I thought you did not see me. How did you know who I am?

For the first time he laughed and his guffaws resonated like an echo because of the ether. With his laugh, the space vibrated, reverberated as if the joyfulness were the one that dilated and contracted the celestial bodies, those particles of the Universe. Cometa produced in me the same sensation as the jacaranda when I formed part of its sap.

— I have known you since you were a child —he explained, still laughing.

I doubted he knew about my past so I preferred to ask him about what he called "universal life".

— Why do you say that the animated and unanimated matter is the same?
— The fast spaces of light are guided by the principle that says: In the union of the matter the equality is found —he answered.
— How would you explain that principle?

The old man seemed not to have listened to my question. When he noticed his distraction, he looked at us again with his strange and colour-of-light eyes. Meanwhile, we were wrapped by the lukewarm of the honeycomb nucleus of the comet.

5

"I have known you since you were a child", Cometa insisted. I did not succeed in distracting his attention and he began saying:

"You were born, in the presence of the Sun and with full moon, at six o'clock in an unfinished December day the twenty second. A few months earlier, your father had disappeared. He was accused of being a sorcerer; that is why they followed him. Tlilal, your mother, took refuge near a meandering fall of water and she spilled in the river her tears in cluster. After giving birth, she remained sick and weak. Being afraid of dying, she let the river took care of you and she left looking for her couple. That is why your name is Yauh, which means 'to leave'. Hoping that someday the three of you would meet, with thorns of maguey and tint of the flowers of jacaranda mixed with the purple snails, she tattooed a Y on your chest, at the side of the heart. You still keep that tattoo, which you always knew was a mole and that also your father has, although in another part of his body".

Tao and Huitzil remained far away, watching the fertilizing labour of the comet; I felt disconcerted, it worried me to continue on the old man's side, sowing life and sowing matter.

> — How difficult Tlilal's search is —I told him with indifference.
> — The night she left, the intermittent light of fireflies that ascended forming the words "yauh, yauh" accompanied her. That night, like all the ones of full moon, the dance of the fireflies glowed; they welcomed you that way.
> — Why do you relate them with me?
> — As they cannot return with their mothers, the stars, the fireflies have the gift that some of their wishes are fulfilled in their tears. They always yearned to receive an emissary from the stars; they wanted to be loved. In you, they saw their wish fulfilled, which is why they called you Andoreni, "the one who came from the firmament". Since you were a little boy, they have been close to you, along with the jacaranda, in which you nurtured yourself of joyfulness.
> — I still do not understand.
> — Since you were born at six o'clock, time in which neither it is day nor night, your nature is hybrid, as long as you equally received

influence from both the Sun and the Moon. This particularity makes you capable of loving and be loved by all form of universal life. Life is given to the day you are born, and that day ends with the disappearance of the one that gave it. Your day has not finished yet.

I did not want to know more about my origin, I felt fear, and I said it to Cometa, but he warned me that with such distrust, I would not be able to go deeper in the spaces of light and he carried on his story.

"I think the fear comes from the time you were at risk of losing the life. When you were just a few months old, a coral snake bit your left leg. The injury, about to become gangrenous, healed thanks to the massages with filaments of a fuzzy spiky red flower called callistemon and the rubber of castor-oil plant that the iguanas applied. Prone and with fever, if not by the nectar with which the huitzils fed you, surely you would have died.

"You stood on your own feet and needed to fish in order to feed you —he continued—, a hawk attempted to grab what you had captured and upon impeding it hurt your left temple. With aquatic plants, you cured your injury until it healed. This was the second time that, as a child, you were going to die. The third one happened because you were used to play with the current of the river and in a backwater swam toward the shore. One time, it was high, you ignored the risk and it dragged you until you ended up stuck by the neck in the forked stick of some branches fallen into the water. Because of the pressure of the branches, and in spite of the few minutes that went by, the apple of Adam deviated toward right. A tall and thin shepherd, of enigmatic appearance named Pacindo, was coming gathering the goats of his flock when he saw something swaying in the river. He supposed it was an otter; he withdrew his dagger and cautiously approached hoping to catch it. However, what would not his amazement be, when at waving the weapon he detected you. Upset due to his finding, he decided to take care of you in his hut, where your recovery was difficult. During weeks, at night you woke up terrified, breathing with trouble, almost with asphyxia. Pacindo assisted your illness with an aromatic smoke of herbs that collected in the mount, but you were never allowing to move away too much in search of them; since you only repeated 'yauh, yauh', with the expression of terror in your out of orbit eyes you obliged him to remain with you.

"During the nights, next to a fire, looking toward the east he expected your improvement; at that time, the flames projected the shade of the wise shaman until confusing it with the mountain. He was attracted to loneliness, you to the river, and guided by the confidence, every day you were getting closer to its border. You kept on repeating 'yauh, yauh'; until actually you left and never met again. Because of that hidden fear, since you were a child you were attracted to the desert and in its stuffy silence your past was lost".

6

Through the old man's story, drops in cluster flew from our eyes, which also spread in the Universe. The celestial body in which we travelled seemed to cry detaching fragments and, little by little, it approached to its extinction; maybe that is why Cometa became silent.

> — To what will our tears give origin, as sad as we are? —Huitzil asked.
> — Perhaps to beings product of our desires, as it happens with the fireflies —Tao said—, other forms of universal life may cry like dew and spread theirs in this way.

Guided by Cometa and attracted by the waterfall, we arrived just to the place where the torrent swallowed us. Pensive, we did not realize when the old man hid.

I took Tao and Huitzil to the origin of the roads and showed them the tunnel that leads to the place of inner secrets, by which I could return to my habitual world but they stopped me and we preferred to enter in the second road of the spaces of light, which looked of easy trajectory.

As soon as we had lost sight of the place of departure, we were left dark. Nevertheless, it was strange that we heard perfectly well and did not feel any fear.

> — Where are we? —Tao asked with the firmness of his clear voice, sounding released from a deep enclosure.

"This road brought you to the spaces of the personal experiences —said someone whose voice created a melody in each word and that invited to enjoy it and hope it did not finish—. This is the space where the spiritual substance is found of those who are or were deaf-mutes. They live and learn through the sight, which is why upon arriving to their cosmic space they prefer not to see, and to hear and speak perfectly well instead".

> — What is your name? —Huitzil asked.
> — My name is Voz —and by the pleasant sonority of her utterance, she made us understand that from that word the chant had been born.

— Are you deaf-mute also? —I asked her with my peculiar melancholic tone.
— That is right —Voz answered—, most of the time I live here, where I can speak and delight myself with the sounds I hear now. This experience calms me down and when I go back to the habitual world I feel joyful of being as I am and of enjoying my eyes.
— And when you are in this world how is your inner talk? —we asked her with a pitch of voice whose resonance recalled the uproar of the water in cascade.
— In our inner silence, the secret of the music is hidden.

At that moment, we realized that the darkness of that cosmic space trembled with a tenuous musical background, which accompanied the melody of our talk. We made a rest and the silence made the sound got closer. The *allegro* of an unknown symphony was heard; whose silences and sounds enjoyed their sudden freedom.

— Why is this symphony heard? —I asked Voz.
— The feeling of this composition allows us to relieve the rancour because our words are not heard and its strength propitiates we alleviate our sadness. Besides, we are proud of knowing that music was born for this cosmic space; from the first compositions, their destiny was always to arrive here, just a few creators have known about it.
— And why is the darkness of this space?
— The sound and the silence are like the light and the shade: inseparable. The sound is the light of the silence and the shade is the silence of the light. Why seeing if we hear? Why hearing if we see?

I listened to the symphony attentively and its naturalness made me feel the fraternity and harmony of all that has been created.

I comprehended perfect chords guide the cosmos and the creations known on Earth are a smallest part of that incessant symphony of the Universe that is yet to be written.

7

We let us be guided by the music and, from the complete darkness, abruptly, we passed to another space where you could see with dazzling neatness or maybe it was that we recovered the sight; as fast as these facts happened. In that place, our thoughts and sensations were materialized in what happened.

We got thirsty and an eye of water appeared whose diaphanous bubbling emerged among shining garnet rocks. We anxiously drank and the satisfaction was so complete that made us feel that we would not have that avidity again. Nevertheless, the water was cold, strangely cold and it brought us memories, thirst of our past.

Tao remembered his experience in the desert and he wanted to get his weapon back; it was this way he got the most solid lance of ivory out of all the ones he had displayed, but it did not emit any fire when he moved it with his habitual dexterity.

The spring made me think of Tlilal and by remembering her, the most attractive essence of woman arrived before us. She awoke by her delicacy the temptation of possessing her, but she lacked warmth. Her presence filled us of lust but not of joyfulness.

Huitzil undertook the flight and it was not enough to him to do it with his habitual agility, but, on having opened the wings, it was generating intense tonalities which twinkles were forming a numberless of rainbows in fan. Huitzil not only was flying, his displacements resembled a dance. That was, his sudden turning and the hanging plumage were creating a dance; but it was not impressive, it was an icy dance. Huitzil was so entertained by the tonalities of his rainbows that I tried to flight, but the only thing that I achieved was to do rhythmic movements.

> — Exactly, that is correct —suddenly told me the attractive feminine essence—. We like to dance because when we do it we feel the flight.

We were perplexed at noticing her words sounded the same, none of them expressed the nuances of affection; she only transmitted us her coldness. She gave us her kindness. "What will happen to us if we remain here?" For thinking about it, we lost our affective experiences. It was us, but different; we ended up as cold beings the same as her. "But what cosmic space is this one?" We should not have asked it either, because she immediately answered us:

"You are in the space of the uncreated. Where what is born from the imagination or the desire and was never created, is found in perfect state. The only condition is that what is pictured or desired is original. That which could come into existence remained like a rigid essence, along with the personal affective experiences that cause. Here you can find the work of art that was not carried out. The scientific discovery that was not done, the possible technical advance, the repressed mystic experience, the philosophic idea that was not concluded, the loving experience without germinating, the essence of those beings that could not be born and the creative expressions that remained suspended in the imagination or in the desire".

— And why is it here the essence of what has not been created? —Huitzil asked.
— It is because there is love in this space.
— What love?
— It is the love that did not germinate.
— Are you the source of love? —Tao asked.
— No, I am Desamor —she said smiling with a cold sweetness.
— But how is it? —Tao exclaimed.
— I am the essence of dislove, waiting for each of the not-born essences and, perhaps, myself, will be called because of an act of creative love.
— But if some day you were created it would be disastrous —Huitzil said.
— It has happened like this —and she smiled again.
— The risk is that the dislove is not envied, from here that there is no one to stop it. That is why, do not fall in love with her and let us go —Tao said, alarmed.

8

Nothing convinced us and we insisted on remaining in the cosmic space of the uncreated. Or rather, that is what I wanted.

> — Let us go, Yauh —Tao insisted, by so doing, unfortunately he made disappear the beautiful essence.
> — I want to keep on admiring Desamor —I answered him.
> — But how can you be interested in a woman without warmth? — Huitzil said.
> — Why did you have to speak? She disappeared because of your blame.
> — I did not think you were so much interested in her —Tao said.
> — And you were not? Why do you keep your lance, then?
> — It is not for Desamor that I have this lance; besides, without fire, I am not interested in it —he added, breaking it without any difficulty—. Look, it is made of ditch reed; it is useless for me.
> — I am sure that Huitzil likes forming the rainbows of ice.
> — My flight no longer forms a rainbow; I do not have to stay here either.

I felt betrayed by them and I felt they lied. I thought they wanted to continue in the space of the uncreated, but they wanted to leave because Desamor was mine; or maybe they tried I left and to stay with her.

> — It is all right let us going! —I told them.
> — Go-ahead —they answered me, when the garnet already had the appearance of volcanic stone.

We began to go away, but actually, I wanted to look for her. I walked with apparent decision, while thinking how to get rid of them. I pretended to be watching an anthill thoroughly and when I wanted to reach them, an inexplicable fatigue stopped me, every time more intense. Tao and Huitzil got ahead, on the other hand, my legs did not react and my arms hung bent. I thought about asking them for help, but I did not want to receive any favours, I did not want to humiliate myself before them. I tried to take a step and I fell in a bank of sand; every time I tried to escape I sank more, up to that prison took possession of half of my body. Again, I wanted to shout to them so they rescue me and what I said was "Desamor, help me!"

Immediately, very close to the anthill, I felt impregnated of sand and it petrified me. A whirl agitated wrapping. "Those are not friends —I thought—; if they were they would come to help me". The gusts of the whirl threw the ants against my body, which went over it biting it and caused me an unbearable burning. "Desamor, Desamor!" I begged so she came; but my voice did not seem to be heard. In contrast, I heard that somebody, or maybe everything, shouted at me: "Go away, go away!"

The hail began to hit my hard body, making it marshy. Before being left reduced to a heap of mud, the ants fled. "My supposed friends did the same, but Desamor will save me, I am sure about that; she is my allied", I told myself. My destruction was imminent: the avalanche of a river of lava came toward me. "Where are you Desamor?" I shouted, crying of impotence. Her silence made me suspect that Tao and Huitzil would be with her, enjoying her beauty, which maybe they convinced her of going away without helping me, and Desamor, condescending, would have allowed to wrap herself by those nasty fellows. Suddenly, when my tears entered in contact with the sand they opened a hole that made me fall into the void. I did not resist more; I wanted to die. I was going to crash against a rocky prominence, but the fury made me recover the strength and immediately I was climbing a stairway that the more I advanced the more steps it had. At the top, lying on the iron handrail, Desamor, Tao and Huitzil laughed loudly and shouted: "Get out of here, get out of here!" I preferred to go back and similarly there appeared more and more steps to descend. Exhausted, I tried to sit down and there was a scorpion on the step; I decided to jump the handrail and I found myself running disorderly within a passageway of asphyxiating narrowness. I got anxious about its walls with pointed stones that at my passing tore me shreds of skin. It was barely illuminated by distant rays of light, interrupted by a door that opened and closed obeying the erratic will of the wind. The injuries of my feet demanded I stopped, but I had to reach the exit and the fastest I ran, the more narrow the passageway became. From time to time I crossed entrances of other aisles, that started in straight angle, identical to which I travelled by and that called me to go out through them. I saw Desamor, from behind and going away; this alarmed me and I could run with more energy. I thought I would be caught before reaching the exit, which was a small door now, every time smaller and it did not open for me. At the last attempt, I could go out, just to find myself in a flat and straight road.

Exhausted, I collapsed. "Where will Tao and Huitzil be? Surely, they will have seduced Desamor; if I catch them, I kill them; but no, she is not like that. She should be faithful to me and she will refuse any attempts they make to get closer", I thought. I wanted to rest and I did not succeed in seeing, neither in the distance nor at the sides, the end of the road; one had to remain on it all the time. Something startled me. From the horizon, a black point approached. Upon approaching, a noise was heard. A bit later, an enormous ball was coming toward me. The road resounded crushed by the passing of that colossal sphere of stone. I wanted to flee, but the insolent threat did not leave any crack. I tried to look for the passageway entrance, but now nettles and thistles blocked it. Everywhere all I saw was road, the same road, and the sphere, the immense sphere; that insignificant I felt. The roar became unbearable. "I hate you, Desamor!" I yelled horrified and the rock disappeared.

I did not know why I shouted that, if they were whom I felt to hate. I got scared for what I said and I feared that Desamor were disappointed of me. "Because of those ones I am going to lose her", I thought disappointed.

Abruptly, a storm reached me; I had to choose between retreating and taking shelter or advance toward the place where the rain was coming. I decided to face the hurricane; the wind threw lashes of water that hurt my face. I felt fever; sometimes I thought to see, at the distance, Tao and Huitzil, but I thought I was delirious. Exhausted and overcome I sheltered in the hollow trunk of a tree. The storm abated. Still with fever, without knowing if it was by day or at night, I continued walking until I took shelter in a hut of branches and shrubs. Leaning on the straw, I fell asleep with the memory of Pacindo.

When I woke up, the calm company of the vegetation surrounded me. I wanted to go away and I heard them shouting: "Hurry up Yauh, do not insist, do not be stubborn!" That is what Tao and Huitzil said; the free ones by nature, I had better pay attention to them.

9

I approached Tao and Huitzil pretending indifference and with the desire of investigating if they knew about the unfortunate moments, I went through. For their absent-minded attitude, I was convinced that for them I had always been near and there was not any conflict among us. That calmed me down, although as never before, just in that moment, I missed the routine habitual world that I had so much despised.

— Look! —Huitzil told us, while holding something in its beak.

In that moment, it compressed what it had and disintegrated it in a flood of luminous particles that spread, until almost disappear, and then get integrated again. Tao picked up a stone and unintentionally he undid it, just as Huitzil had done with the little stones. It was a shining and fragile space, where the bodies transmitted brightness to each other.

— Yauh, come, let us get into the river —Tao invited me.

When Tao submerged until the knees, the water opened forming furrows. The flow was of light and could interrupt its current easily. The impact of the water of light on the objects was very slight, almost imperceptible. We discovered a colony of giant oysters with appearance of nests of water, out of which pearls of diverse nuances and sizes sprouted. Pearly and multiform bodies formed the flow in a bunch: pearls of water with heart of light.

Like a game, we submerged opening cracks, true abysses in the current and in the bed of the river. In those spaces the sprinkle of light formed, by our interference, universes in which we floated supported by beams of the same brightness, then to return slowly to the original position.

— Come —Huitzil called us—, approach to this forest of light.

In that landscape rigidity did not exist nor attachment to the form: the yellow flowers of the aphelandra could transform into the umbels vermilion of the wayfaring tree and from this to surge the impressionistic stain of the joyful amaranth. From the juvenile rhododendrons, with their compact corymbs, it grew an ahuehuete covered by white long hair given by the hay. Tired of floating in the swamp, the aquatic iris was anchored in its brooks forming an arched mangrove swamp. From the fragrance of the camomile, the most velvet orchid emerged, with petals of edges like a mountain range that were lakes of light and sensuality.

Everything was of water of light. The untiring beaver became a marine serpent and then into a determined salmon that jumped remounting the current. The bears, which lurked the acrobatic jumps of the fish, took us to Polar Regions where we were not cold. The frozen water of light was lukewarm and in the mouth effervesced until melting.

However, even more impressive was that plants, animals and inert shapes, equally, exchanged their form. A tall elm ran transformed into a giraffe, the cautious beetles awoke from the pieces of obsidian and the rocks of marble were born from the bison at rest. The animate and inanimate beings shared a same essence; they were example of the changing universal life.

— Try to lead this orchestra —Huitzil invited us.

We admired it conducting, on one hand, the melodious sway of a group of polychrome butterflies and, on the other hand, the audacious fugues of the dragonflies. There it was represented the impetuousness and the soft grace, under the control of an original director. However, we knew that they were only diverse forms of water of light.

"The eyes are done out of water-light —Tao told us—. That is why they can create and recreate, without any difficulty, all the possible images. With them, we transform them in objects of humid light. We can appear and make disappeared them, integrate and disintegrate them, according to our eyes' taste. Not only plants and animals, but also the inert beings have vision, they capture the world that surrounds them. We see and we are seen. Without a doubt this is the cosmic space of the images".

— Now I understand —I told them—, how Cometa managed to discover me in your nature.
— What do you mean?
— What happened was that he captured me with the light emitted by his eyes, creating my image in that way.

We approached the river where our interference formed universes, when a ship that released sudden blazes crossed in front of us, and with the name, Zirat, inscribed at the prow. At the deck stood out, in spite of the distance, an elder, like an old sun, which lit white tunic was confused with his beard and hair dishevelled.

— Desamor, there goes Desamor! —Huitzil exclaimed.
— Cometa, Cometa! —I shouted at him, but he passed by without answering.

Tao looked at us disconcerted because to him nobody was on the ship.

10

We ran after the ship. As we were going away from the cosmic space of the images, the colour of that which surrounded us was vanishing and it was every time more difficult to distinguish any object.

— What are you running for? We are not going to reach her —Tao said.
— Desamor wants me to follow her —Huitzil said.
— It is Cometa, do not stop —I insisted to Tao.
— What for? It seems ridiculous to me! —he protested.
— If you do not like it, shut up and go away! —I told him.

The confusion of images was also reflected in our loss of control. Just getting the discussion started, Huitzil, challenging, threatened us with the beak.

— Because of your stubbornness, you are acting the clown! —Tao shouted to me, when the ship was already going too far.
— You are a boaster and you think you are invincible! —I answered him.

Huitzil looked at me with hatred and I was afraid of him rushing at me, but unexpectedly he attacked Tao and hurt him in the face. For defending himself, Tao removed part of its plumage. We were willing to disintegrate us.

— Wretched bird! I am going to kill you like the bull! —Tao threatened it.
— Do not be ridiculous, without me you could not have defeated it, you are alive thanks to I put the eyes out! —Huitzil said.
— Pair of idiots! The two of you survived because I formed part of you!
— Because of you I could not fly fast and the bull was about to destroy me! Stupid!
— You are only getting in everybody's way! —Tao told me.
— Idiots! You are ungrateful! —I shouted just when Huitzil hurled against me, scattering feathers for the violence he did it and hurt me in the back. Upon seeing it plucked, I made fun of it and with rage, I told it: treacherous, I hope you die!
— What a pity you did not remain with that witch! You had rotted there! —Tao shouted, and suddenly, he attempted to give me a punch.

It did not matter that every time we insulted each other, our body, tortured by sadness, wasted away in beams of light. We hated each other and it was uncontrollable the impulse of attacking each other.

— I cannot stand you either damned Huitzil! —Tao burst—. I do not know why I saved you from the honeycomb where you were caught! Surely, you have already forgotten it! I had better thrown you to the ants so that they finish with you, when you were desperate trying to remove the honey from you! That torture is the one you deserve now, liar!
— Shut up, slave of the demon! —Huitzil shouted—. Who helped you to escape from the coffee plantations where you were exploited? Who saved you from been taken prisoner by a tribe and being cut up? You have nothing to reproach me the liar is you!
— Go out of here, if you do not want me to destroy you by a slap, foul bird! —Tao groaned, fragile and weakened, as long as they exasperated me even more.
— You are not free at all! You were born to obey, unfortunately I found you! —I told them.
— And what do you boast about, if you are just a miserable liar? —Tao said.
— If I had known who you are, I had never approached you! —I shouted at him, while I felt my own extinction.

We shut up because we lacked strength to attack us. The only thing I could understand was that because of doing mockery of some facts of our past the beams of light of our experiences escaped (except, maybe, the one of sadness), until, weakened, we lost memory, we started becoming transparent and ended up being reduced to our primitive universal essence, that fused in just one being.

11

Crumbled the memory of our experiences until losing the individual substance, without understanding what was going on, the fused being we shared was diluted in the space of the universal essences, where everything was transparent. We remained without age and we stopped watching us.

To my confusion, I was myself, but I was also the rest. I was Yauh, but at the same time Tao and Huitzil. I was equally powder, moss, vapour or tapir; I could be aroma, tide, planet, shade or bamboo. Without meaning it, I was mahogany, desire, lichen, diamond or cotton; ephemeral or perennial, he or I, thought or heat, rock or quince, river or root. What surrounded me was in it, in the individual, but it was also all, in the universal, as fragile as that the individualities resulted.

Crystalline forms out of which their silhouettes were hardly distinguished with original colours in the contours, pleats and prominences represented the ambience. In the phitonias, their plasticity could be admired, with soft green at the edge of the leaves and whitish tones in the nervation. The gladiolas showed their yellow contours and long stalks of an intense green almost imperceptible.

The bodies seemed solid, liquid or gaseous, although they were not, they were in another physical unknown state instead, the one of light, the one of the spaces of light.

In this space, the yes and the no stopped being opposed and they united in a same way of existing. Flying was the most common and impossible, because upon seeing what was seen could be reached. As if we could see from inside and from outside of what we were seeing or rather we formed part of that what surrounded us. In the distance, we looked at a transparent mountain, with its crown of clouds. Its interior was even clearer than the surface, without opacities too. It was a mountain of bubbles, of giant and diaphanous bubbles, whose foamy lumps were visible rocks from the side that as they were watched facing forward they blurred. The roots of the trees looked like the current of an underground river with its tributaries, while the foliage was swaying in eruption of greenish water.

We found a flock of zebras that, upon superposing their contours of soft fringes, shaped mobile fans that sometimes looked like multiple squared chessboards, and then to form again fans in motion. For a moment, the zebras remained one after another and, from the closest to the most distant, a crystalline funnel was formed with walls of white and black mosaics, alternate or lined up. The image invited to enter her and rush to the bottom without limits of that funnel of zebras. When we looked toward the interior of that white and black volume, we found the horizon very close and upon turning the look toward the left side, the right side interposed us. Upon touching the funnel, we fell to the void and when we wanted to escape from its interior, it took us more inside, floating.

At a very short distance, we noticed a transparent moon of a discreet mauve colour. From a vitreous sun close to that moon, sprouted messages that extinguished when they caressed it.

It was an unpredictable flow of forms and counter forms. What existed there appeared and disappeared, without opposites or tunes, it was a cosmic space that modified constantly, leaving us only the reflex of what we had seen. Everything mixed with everything, following capricious transformations of what was a same elemental and elusive substance. However, it included us without any possibility of resisting and we participated of that space with an imperturbable naturalness.

Up to our fused being dispersed in fragments and I no longer knew who I was, if I was something, it did not seem to me important to know it either.

12

We had stopped being what we were. Our being lost its harmony and ended up divided into fragments of light that were dispersed. Our presence was ignored, as well as our opinion. We even soon forgot what it was to have presence or opinion like. Empty of thoughts and emotions, we lost the customary conscience. The last attempts to act or to decide turned out awkward and nonsense. We remained in such a state, if so can be called, indefinable and maybe even of non-existence.

Stopping being what we were was a relief; it separated us from the unpleasant quotidian events. We cared about nothing and nobody cared about us, we got lost in a condition of lamentable in-transcendence. In the chaos of our being, in spite of the entire freedom, we felt broken in fragments of nothing; in comparison to what we were, we were nothing!

Since, upon losing our memory of personal experiences, Tao, Huitzil and I remained fused, in an attempt for explaining what happened to us, the dispersed fragments of our being had, among them or who knows well to whom or to what, the following polyloquy. It was an encounter of nothing with nothing.

— What or who are you?
— I am nothing; sometimes what and sometimes who.
— What is your name?
— It is different every time.
— Why?
— Because I am essence.
— Of what?
— Of everything, I am universal essence.
— Is that to be nothing?
— To be nothing is a state of the being.
— What is it all about?
— In nothing, the essence of the being is the nothing.
— What characterizes it?
— Nothing.
— But are you universal essence?
— Yes!
— Then why are you nothing?

— The universal essence is the nothing that forms part of everything.
— Of all that exists?
— That is how it is: all is nothing. Every being is being nothing.
— But what are you as nothing?
— At a certain moment: nothing!
— And at the next moment?
— Nothing!
— Are you always the same?
— Always!
— But are you different?
— Always!
— And are you nothing?
— Always!
— How is that explained?
— It is not explained.
— Why?
— For being broken in fragments of nothing.
— Are you in everything?
— In all and in nothing!
— Is all, nothing?
— It contains the nothing.
— What does it contain?
— The universal essence.
— How is it?
— Like light that when it turns off, it becomes light again...

13

Our nothing arrived to the mountain of bubbles. By trails translucent crossed a numberless of watery and multi-coloured stones. The roots of the wild plants formed a reticular mantel which rather than nurture from the mountain, they seemed to feed it and support it instead.

Without expecting it, a hillside-mirror revealed us that the eyes of the fused being we shared were kept intact. From that pair the lively and iridescent eyes of Huitzil came off, so the big and impenetrable of Tao did, and mine stayed, still sad. The three pairs of eyes, defenceless, were displacing suspended in the ethereal ambience from which they formed part.

From our eyes, drops in cluster began to slip away without the distress that usually causes them. The flow of tears went conforming our body up to reconstitute it again, with just the transparency we had after losing the memory of our personal experiences. The mirror gave us back the individuality and we recognized us again. Immediately, sadness overwhelmed us.

> — What are you looking for? —a shepherd that looked after goats asked.
> — To recuperate our memory of personal experiences —I told him.
> — You have it in the eyes and in the sadness.
> — Where?
> — Sadness protects the eyes, in which, whether they see or not, the germ of the memory of personal experiences is kept and the essence of the being. That is why you, thanks to your tears, recuperated your body. You are the same, but different.

Somehow, his words and his serenity comforted us. From his blended transparency, his wavy beard and hair stood out. The old man leaned on in a walking stick, of tiger-looking oak for the beautiful vein of the wood. His eyes, colour of light, were the ones that stood out the most.

> — You understand very well what happens to us —Tao told him.
> — I know the roads you are passing through now.
> — Why were we about to disappear? —Huitzil asked.
> — Because of the quarrel, you had.

— What does it have to do with that? —I asked him.
— Upon denuding your spirit, you attacked the harmony of its essence and separated your being, awaking, this way, the implacable anti-being everyone carries inside.
— And only for attacking us?
— No, it was for making known the secrets of your spirit, kept in your memory of personal experiences, which individualize us and our body forms a part of it. We should protect this component of our being from the rest in order to not to be left in the insubstantial state in which, for your mistake, you ended up.
— Why do we dilute in the space of the universal essences?
— Because you are the same to all that exists. You share the same essence: the light, beginning of the universal life.

His chat made us remember that experience in which we sowed life and sowed matter.

— You look like Cometa —Huitzil noticed.
— I am Pacindo —he said smiling.
— Pacindo? Cometa told us about you. I know what I owe you, thanks for your loving help.
— Well we are here... together again.

I wanted to stay with Pacindo; I tried to convince him. I felt confident next to him, but he refused. Cometa had told us he was lonely by nature.

— If it is not possible for us to remain, I think we should return —Tao interrupted.
— You cannot return as you are.
— Why? —Tao asked him, annoyed.
— You are not what you were anymore; you do not know what you will be: you have to go on.
— What do we have to do? —Huitzil asked, fearfully.
— Go to the mauve moon; get close to it, since you need to pass through its interior.
— And then?
— After passing over it, you will find the eyes of the Universe.
— The eyes of the Universe?
— Yes. They are two vitreous suns: twin suns named Gael and Dael; this road gets up to them. Moreover, always light the lantern of the reflection and of the feeling on.

We looked at each other intrigued. Pacindo wanted us to not only leave, but he also threaten us to confront new risks. However, upon saying goodbye I got the feeling that he watched my destiny.

14

With the naive transparency of our bodies, we went looking for that mauve moon. It was Huitzil who found it. It was hidden behind the mountain, getting confused with it, on the opposite side from where we were. The lunar sphere remained touching the floor. By an opening of its curved surface rushing bubbles slipped away. They either arranged in lumps or fused among themselves forming crystalline spheres more voluminous. Perhaps it had been them which in crowded clusters had formed the mountain. Upon approaching the moon it was born again in us a sensation of joyfulness we had forgotten. Overcoming the fall of the small moons we could enter; we felt a fearful curiosity for what could happen to us.

— A purple forest! —Huitzil shouted suddenly.
— Jacarandas in flower! —Tao said—, and inside the moon!

The flowers gave their colour to the moon and their joyfulness to us. Each one of us was attracted by a certain tree, and I felt seduced by a leafy jacaranda that, on a mound, stood out the others. I decided to get closer. The floor that enclosed its stalk was covered by violet flowers that invited to lie down. I sat down leaning on the trunk; its palpitating bark seemed to communicate with a woman of sweet mauve eyes who was coming toward me. The attractive contours of her transparency were barely covered by a dress of vaporous pale green silk, hugged with elegance to her waist. Her beautiful feet had low-cut shoes that made stand out the forms of her tall body. Her shiny dark chestnut hair was upheld with a silk ribbon. The wind made the dress accentuate her shape, looking even more sensual. I felt full of new emotions and wanted to kiss her.

— My name is Luna —she said with a loving voice—. This is my home; welcome to the house where the inspiration of love is born.
— I am Yauh, I am passing by.
— You may remain if you want to —she invited me, while she caressed my cheek with the back of her hand—. Do not be frightened —she said, upon watching me going quiet. Sitting next to me, she began to play with her hands, insinuating, with the carpet of flowers.

At that moment, flashes surging from a transparent sun that was approaching.

> — How silky your hair is —I told her, and without imagining that she would consent, I caressed it.
> — I would like that the hairs that cover your body were touching mine —she asked me; while braiding her legs with mine. As an answer, my fingers drew on her the caresses of desire.

The solar sphere continued approaching. The flashes were felt more passionate. The flowers of the jacaranda opened full of pride, the mauve became intensified and everything inside the moon was devoted to love.

I undid the knot of the ribbon that fastened the dress to her waist and her body surrendered to my eyes.

> — Your name is a delight, Yauh, and I am attracted to your muscular body —she said in a low voice, while I lay her down on the flowers.
> — Your mauve body turns me on.
> — I like you like that —she whispered and opened her lips to mine.

The vitreous sun was nearer every time and its flashes were more impetuous.

> — How intense the crown of the sun is! —I whispered her at the lips.
> — Its flames are messages of love for the moon —she answered; when the mauve and the orange braided trying to be two and to be one.
> — They look like arms that wrap the moon —I told her while kissing her neck.
> — Hug me in your flames! —she asked me.

The sun reached the moon, and the small moons drained toward the mountain; they were bubbles of love, from the substance love is made. How was it possible —I thought— that love was a substance? Maybe the same substance in that moment gave us form.

> — An eclipse will take place —she told me—, it will accompany ours. The eclipse is the love of the celestial bodies. They hug like this, just as you and I now.

The mauve and the orange were two and one at the same time, like the sun and the moon, and like her and me. I gave her the ring of diamonds from the eclipse and I placed on her temples the crown of luminous filaments of the sun. We joined our bodies, until the illusion of remaining always together put us to sleep.

When I woke up, she was going away concentrating the mauve around her and spreading it in tiny lunar spheres; my revitalized body shared its serenity with the repose of the moon. Tao and Huitzil arrived calmed, as if they had lived a similar experience. We walked toward the other side, where clots of crystalline bubbles were also falling, and we ended just a step from the sun. From there I looked at the cloak of jacarandas in flower, where with reminiscences of our eclipse Jacaranda Luna would be.

15

It seemed to us to see the sun so close that, we thought in order to arrive to it, it would be necessary only to reach its mouth. Upon walking without hesitation toward the image we had of its entrance, the unexpected ocean that separates the two celestial bodies caught us. We sank in that sea and inevitably were dragged by its currents. An involuntary change happened to us since we lost the proportions of our bodies and we expanded up to acquiring cosmic dimensions. As far as I was concerned, I breathed without any difficulty and I looked for my friends to know how they would be.

— We have scales colour of moon! —Huitzil said.
— We are fish! —Tao exclaimed—; transparent fish in the dark ocean of the Universe!

The dragon of the depths in which Tao had turned into showed from the cheekbones and along its flexible body, luminous points that competed with the efforts that the abyssal night made to hide it. Its filamentous beard was used as a helm in order to go on the way he wanted. The ceratias in which Huitzil became, was equally attractive, it displayed a dorsal torch that like a lighthouse orientated us.

— You are surrounded by herrings —Tao told me.

The cosmic deep transformed me into a regaleco with a red tuft of feathers that went over my body. I was surprised to move through undulatory movements, helped by the rhythmic beat of the lateral small swords that originated at the base of my neck. My elastic oars had a fluorescent bulb at the extreme that helped me be guided by the reef of stars. We swam through the ether, by the void of ether, formed of water, ethereal water and confused in it by our jellied transparency.

— An avalanche is seen there —Huitzil said.

Upon going toward it, we found that it was Orion's arm, in the Milky Way. The marine current that originates from the avalanche, took us to visit, in a turbulent race, the Lebrels, the Pleiades, Hydra, the South Cross and other of its areas. We preferred to go even further on, got closer to the galaxies birth, and were surprised to discover that they originate from the fall to the void of a waterfall of sidereal sand that results from the torrents that flow from each of the eyes of the Universe: the twin eyes that Pacindo called Dael and Gael. To them we had to get.

Lost in the intermixed day's run of the celestial bodies, we discovered that some of the luminescent particles of the universal waterfall, when they are dispersed, form, among many others, the constellations we admire from our solar system.

Finally, we succeeded in distinguishing, in perspective, the hive of the twenty-two closest galaxies from ours and whose group forms a whirled bell that through its ringing not only spread its cosmic sand, but also contributes with them to the incessant symphony of the Universe.

From the distance depths, I turned the eyes toward the moon, and like a magnifying glass, its mauve flashes threw the message to the space:

>   Sea
>   to-sea
>   amaranth
> so much love:
>   joyfulness.

— Celestial bodies in duplicate are seen everywhere —Huitzil exclaimed.
— Every celestial body of those that form a pair should have been born from one of the eyes of the Universe —Tao said.

Feeding ourselves of plankton, formed by the sidereal sandy, we wandered lost by shoal of asteroids and by firmaments of water. At Pollux star, that became the anchor for our orientation, we came across a royal moonfish of scarlet fins. It offered to take us up to the mouth of the vanished vitreous sun, after this, it would go back to Pollux. In effect, we did so.

Wishing to leave the cosmic deep and not being fish, we made an effort to approach the sun. Upon turning the eyes, inattentive, to admire the torrent of sidereal sand for last time, we remained caught in a net of threads of silk that carried fluorescent light. Each knot of the net was formed by a bright bloom like a star, from its interior countless filaments were released which in all directions made more extensive the tetradimensional mantle of the incandescent mesh.

We decided to approach to one of those blooms and found the effervescent emergence of the cords of light, but we could not enter. Leaning on one of those shiny nests, we noticed the interlaced filaments made a constellation that protected the entrance of the vitreous sun.

> — Let us try to pass for a flower bud —Huitzil insisted.

It was useless. The only thing we got was being more entangled, without knowing what was happening within that warp of silk.

> — Only through one of the flower buds we will succeed in arriving to the sun —Tao said.

Because of the rays of light, made out of silk, I remembered Jacaranda Luna, since the net and the flower buds had the same pale green colour of her dress. "Let us respond to her message of love" —I told them—, and we were devoted to the task of knitting her name with the threads of that constellation, up to finishing the generation of threads and reeling one of the skeins.

When at last we succeeded in undoing the hank, many tiger-butterflies came out to impede us to pass. They are in charge of not letting anybody to get close to the entrance of the sun. In addition, occupying that home, we found marine caterpillars, of white skin and dark spots.

> — What do you want? —a caterpillar asked us, while weaving the weave of its house, producing quickly a gummy liquid from which the luminous fibbers originated.
> — We would like to enter the sun —I told them.
> — Since you succeeded in opening the weave, you can do it, but before finishing spinning —it answered us abruptly, and the butterflies let us enter.
> — What constellation do you form? —Tao asked them.
> — It is the Silk Swarm constellation, twinned with the Quiordea and Rualá constellations, also unknown for you —it answered and we said goodbye.

We passed the net. When we were leaving the cosmic sea, just a bit was needed to stop being fish, and at last we arrived to the vitreous sun: one of the twin eyes of the Universe.

16

Helped by the generating ambience of life that enclosed the vitreous sun, without stopping being transparent, each one of us recuperated his original form. At its entrance, a pearly-looking slippery pending stopped us. We arrived to the summit with difficulty and, when sliding toward the interior of the sun, we started getting into a spiral labyrinth. One of his inclined facings, like a slide, threw us to a beach that let it be invaded by a sea in flames. However, it was a calm sea, with discreet waves, but of fire, all of fire. In some places of rested water, it looked like honey in their appearance. With pleasure, we fed from her and, especially, it nurtured our mind, causing us an unusual form of thinking.

Orange snails covered the beach and inside the water in flames, there were of diverse sizes; there were also tree-shaped chorals of the same shade.

> — The orange of many snails and chorals of the Earth tell their origin —Tao said.
> — Where is Huitzil? —I asked.
> — Huitzil! —Tao shouted.
> — Here! —he answered us.

He was at the top of the concavity of the sun, lying on what looked like an immense lamp of lighting red, orange and yellow brightness. He seemed amused picking the multiple fountains of light and at doing it; he splashed sparks and twinkles that were dispersed.

> — What are you doing Huitzil? —Tao asked.
> — I am eating! —he shouted to us.
> — What are you eating?
> — Yes, I am eating tejocotes; they are delicious!
> — Tejocotes? —we asked.
> — Yes, together with capulín berries, they are the most delicious fruit that there is! —he insisted us.

Watching carefully toward Huitzil was, we found out that from the profound of the concavity of the sun an enormous fruit-covered tree hung. It was a tejocote, but I seemed upright and upside down at the same time. Its roots, like a veined waft, spread from the centre to the sides of the dome of the sun and from here, a powerful trunk came off. It gave origin to a leafy tree illuminated by its exquisite fruit.

> — Look, there are tejocotes on the beach! —Tao remarked me.
> — The tejocotes become into snails! —I commented him.

Actually, the tejocotes, as well as many snails, are like small suns of a colour that goes from intense red like the sun of dawn or it that lies on the sea, to the pale yellow of the sun of zenith, going through all the tones of orange.

> — Then the tejocotes of the solar tree should give origin to the multiple suns of the Universe —Tao commented.
> — And the ones that do not give origin to a sun, must remain like snails spread in all the worlds, carrying on the drawings of their shell the cosmic plan that if we deciphered it, it might tell us the exact place where they come from —I told him.

I remained pensive and I smiled because of the astonishment that it caused me to learn that the sun was just an enormous tejocote... Maybe that is why the tejocotes, to offer heat, give fruit only in winter.

The cicadas were right, I thought, here they remain vestiges of solid rays and, besides, it is found the origin of the enigmatic snails scattered on the ocean and beaches of infinity of worlds. Carrying hidden in their cuirass the impossible desire of returning to the sea of fire where they come from.

> — The pendant by which we slide is just the mouth of an enormous snail and its spiral the labyrinth where we go deeper —Huitzil said.
> — Look you at the dome, it seems a honeycomb —Tao said.
> — Watch out, a giant wave! —Huitzil shouted, when the water of fire already soaked us and the reddish foam left on the beach.
> — What is this? —Tao asked.
> — From the foam of the sea fireflies come out, they must be mother fireflies —I told them, seeing them raising the flight like luminous rain.
> — Where will they go? —Huitzil asked.
> — Follow them and we will reach you!
> — There they come down; they gather somewhere! —he told us in a hurry.

We ran enthusiastically following Huitzil and, upon arriving, he was waiting for us next to a spring where the generation of inflamed honey colour water was endless.

— A diagram, I saw a diagram inscribed on a tombstone! —Huitzil shouted.
— Where?
— At the bottom of the spring.
— What is it like?

Huitzil, with his beak, drew on the honey sand the mysterious diagram that from the heights he had discovered at the bottom of the spring.

— Like this:

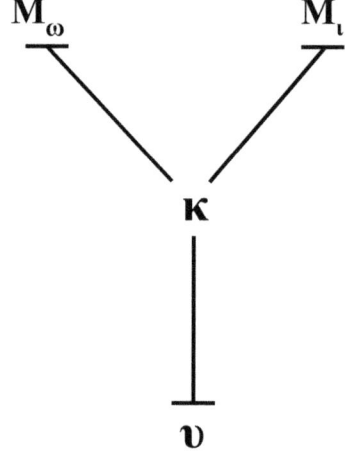

— What will it mean? —Tao asked.
— I would like to know it —Huitzil said.
— They look like Greek letters at the ends and in the centre of a Y —I told them.
— They must mean something —Tao said.
— Maybe they have a relationship with the principle that Cometa did not want to explain to us —I reminded them.

Studying the diagram caused that, suddenly, we discovered to each body its double.

We saw superimposed images, not only of ourselves but also including the interior of the sun. That is why Pacindo called them twin suns: we were in both at the same time.

Intrigued, we observed thoroughly the diagram, wondering what its meaning would be, until Tao told us:

— I have an idea; perhaps it may help us to begin to understand the diagram.
— What is it?
— M_ω could symbolize live matter and M_t the inert —he answered.
— And what about the κ?
— Perhaps it refers to the light speed, main characteristic of the spaces we have visited.
— And the υ may represent the union of both forms of matter —I added.
— This would mean that as the matter, live or inert, approaches the speed of light, it will behave the same way, no matter what properties it has at rest —Tao added.
— Of course! That is why Cometa talked about the equality resulting from the union of the matter —I told them.
— Yauh, what other way would you expresses what the diagram says? —Huitzil asked.
— Maybe it refers —I told them— to the organic matter m_o and the inorganic m_i, at the speed of light c, tend to standardize in their properties U:

$$U = (m_o + m_i)c$$

Equation I wrote on the honey sand, next to the diagram Huitzil drew.

— It is the same if it is said that, at the speed of light, $m_o = m_i$ —Huitzil said.

Because our way of thinking and expressing was not the habitual, we did not trust the validity of our conclusions, but it was more important the emotion they caused us. However, the body and the spirit of our being felt in an independent way and each one transmitted us their own perceptions. Perhaps that is why; we were still seeing everything in duplicate.

— Will we be right?
— We cannot know it... that might be the meaning of the diagram —Tao said.
— The only thing that seems clear is that, in the spaces of light, there is no difference between the living and the inert... as if at that speed everything was becoming into spirit —I told them.

By that time, the pores of our body had already been impregnated with spirit; we felt in internal harmony. Finding the diagram and discussing its possible meaning, helped us to get rid of the prejudices that separate the living from the inert and thanks to that, our being was integrated. The moon vitalized it; the twin suns gave it spirit: we stopped seeing and feeling double.

We remained watching the flaming spring, guarded by leafy cactuses of fire, especially the dart type. These gave the impression of being looking after the puzzle. In the sea, formed by drops in cluster, millions of new fireflies were being gestated.

> — This is the source of life! —we said in unison.
> — And of the matter!
> — Of the universal life!

We approached the crowd that gave origin to the spring. "How I would like to know who guides the fireflies", I thought, captivated by that sight.

> — Listen, it is the dance of the fireflies; there will be a colour-honey water storm —Huitzil said.

From the vault of the sun, like an immense honeycomb in the shape of a lamp, countless bunched together drops drained and joined the current of the spring from which the sea was nourished, so to give origin to more fireflies.

Their dance intensified, another gigantic wave washed the beach and from its foam, more fireflies surged. Some of them were integrated to the beautiful solar lamp, but many others came out from its interior and like fragments of sun went to other places to sow universal life.

> — There must be a queen firefly here —Tao said.
> — One or many —Huitzil added frightened, since the place reminded him of that experience when he ended up caught in a honeycomb.
> — Every beehive of the Earth is like a sun and the honey the most delicious sample of the water of fire. Bees look like fireflies that have stopped cry —Tao said—. I would like to go deeper into this honeycomb.
> — Of course! —I told him.
> — I would rather get out of here and be again, where the roads meet —Huitzil complained.
> — Look at your skin —I told Tao—, when you fought with the bull the colour of your body was like the one you have now, colour of fire.

Tao smiled of joy and pointed out that Huitzil and I had a similar tone to him.

By then our bodies were more opaque every time. The marks these experiences left in our memories caused that little by little our slaving non-transparency reappeared. We started to earn age.

17

After recovering the original opacity of our bodies, the necessity of returning to the fork of the roads was irresistible; we were looking for the protection of what we knew. Having this purpose, we joined one of the fragments that came off the vitreous sun and as nearing the place where we set off; we were recovering our habitual dimensions. Being already at that place, we ended up in front of the tunnel that comes from the point of the inner secrets.

— I think we have to say goodbye, I would not like to risk any longer —Huitzil suddenly said.
— What do you think? —Tao asked me.
— I would like to be alone.

I went to the tunnel and noticed that its interior consisted of a cylinder of reddish walls, fluffy to the touch and to the steps. I realized a warm wind flows and redounds, making oscillate countless cilia that covered the humid surface. I also had the impression that firmer rings and softer sections formed the tunnel, and like a bellow, it shortens and lengthens softly.

While I was walking toward the tunnel exit I could see with certain clarity, but if I looked toward the back there was a wall of rejecting darkness. That is to say, the entrance to the spaces of light gave brightness to my body and the return to the habitual world took it away. My movements, clumsy again, did not emit beams of light: as well as the tunnel had made me enter; it also pushed me out.

Near my routine ambience, I remembered the limited light of my lamp table, with its over burned screen, the creaks of the wooden chair and the pile of books and left-out papers that made even smaller the space of my little desk. I pictured myself covered by the frayed blanket, which I try to protect myself from my always-cold room. I disliked to see the torn curtains of the narrow window which, heading to the north, prevents the sun's rays from getting in and causes, because of the constant humidity, the books and any object there might be inside to go off, polluting the already little ventilated place. Neither did I want to feel again the cynical look of my tired mirror. For these memories, the sensation of load that tortured me came back. I hesitated on leaving.

I avoided the possibility of meeting myself again. This ambience was sordid to me; the one I visited was incomprehensible. I did not feel to belong to any of them.

I found myself writing in my study. I put my throat on my left hand; by doing this, I seemed to protect the point of the inner secrets, located in the vertex of Adam's apple. The two parts of the apple join there and make a Y when fusing down. I wrote the following story:

The victory

December 22

I was scared by the solitude and abandonment, since I had always felt like that: lonely. Because of the solitude, I never learned to distinguish, because nobody taught me, the good from the bad, or how to live better, exposing me, without a reason, to many risky situations. I was always enclosed in the fantasy of taking shelter in a desert: thoughtful, shy, very shy. Watching people and, to me, their inexplicable reactions. I learned to walk and to speak very late. I was physically weak and when I needed to hit other children, not only did they make fun of me but also I was usually beaten.

Food made me sick very often, that is why I got thinner and thinner. At those times, I was always going to a river and the purity of its water was curing me. The sound of the current, even now, calms me down and when it gets more intense I can anticipate whether there will be rain soon or not.

Every time I tried to go to school, they did not let me in. They did not understand why a nine-year-old child was not able to speak. They were always accusing me of a fool. The biggest ridicule I had was one time that I fell down in a ditch where the sewage from a stable came; everyone laughed at me. The pestilence was unbearable so I ran toward the river, my only refuge. From then on, I moved away from people so that they were not bothering me.

However, the worst was that I did not know anything about religion and people are very religious in towns. I did not understand their prayers neither why they were having their religious festivities so I left. One time, as a teenager, somebody was needed to be punished "for being a sinner" so I was pointed out and shouted at "to that, to that bloody phthisical." By pulling me, they took me with them. I was very frightened: somebody tore my clothes and dressed me with a blanket and huaraches. I had to carry some very heavy and cross-shaped beams. They made me climb a hill by lashing me. In spite of my pleas, some women who were crying never helped me. I fell down and fainted several times, up to I got to the summit at last; they tied me at the cross and put me a crown of thorns of maguey that hurt me up to the point of making my skin bleed. When I ended up like that, faint, they bowed at me. The women continued crying. Before the evening, some drunk men put me down and I remained alone and thrown in the middle of the rain. They did not give me back my clothes. What I did, as soon as I could, was to flee from the town. This was my victory, my elemental victory: escaping, escaping, time after time...

The story was unfinished. I went out to the street, looked at the liquidambars and they seemed to me stronger than usual. Upon joining, their branches they formed a tree-lined dome which because of the time of the year, it showed green, yellow, magenta and brown shades. Their already dry spherical fruit with tens of pointed salient looked like multi-radial light bulbs that emitted stars in series and intermittent light.

Upon walking, in the middle of the avenue, I felt as if I went inside a cathedral of luminescent stained-glass windows. When I arrived to the end of the street where another passage converged, I still walked guarded by those interweaved arches of those trees coloured by the winter. I watched again the bright cup of the liquidambars: they made a Y where the streets met.

Nevertheless, the bright and colourful grove did not excited me, I felt unsatisfied. I disliked my life of enclosure even more and, by the point of the inner secrets, I decided to return to find again my friends.

18

I met Tao and Huitzil at the fork, but now the roads were like any road, it was not seen neither the resplendence of one nor the easy way of the other, my friends were also disappointed. I felt disillusioned and fear of having reappeared the load I was fleeing.

— Yauh! —I was said.

We shared the same disappointment, but I noticed them noncommittal.

— What are you hiding? —I asked them.
— There is a third road. We preferred not to tell you —Huitzil said.
— Aren't you interested in covering it?
— We have that doubt —Tao answered.
— As you like…, but perhaps that is the best that remains for us to do.

The third road was coming from the opposite direction to the others, forming a Y with them. Insecure, we began going by it and soon it took us to the foot of a leafy oak, covered by olive-coloured acorns; the enclosure of that place invited to remain there.

Around a bonfire in which the day left its light, there were placed in circle nine seats of mud, fire-coloured, in groups of three. The place, masterfully prepared by the hands of the Universe, was surrounded by leafy magueys with their mequiotes to the full. To the sides of the oak, two agaves that indeed produced agave juice, aguamiel, were starting a fence. In the middle of these main magueys, there was a wide hollow formed by the dry base of an agave. Although it was almost at night, in the environment stood out many cactuses modelled by the wind.

We sat down in front of the oak, just where the road we had travelled ended; Tao to my left side and Huitzil to the right. The night intensified the bonfire and only the occasional howl of the coyotes disturbed the silence; they sang to the full moon, calling it.

— Look at who is coming! —Huitzil shouted.
— It is Cometa! —Tao said.

Actually, surrounding the oak, Cometa appeared accompanied by two old men: Pacindo and the old Sun, the one of the ship Zirat. They sat down to our left, Pacindo between the other two. The smiling old men's eyes, colour of light, stood out.

— Somebody else is coming —Tao pointed out—, are women.

They were Desamor, Jacaranda Luna and another woman as beautiful as they were, although perhaps older and sad-eyed. Upon sitting down, those ones flanked the oldest. They looked at us affectionately and smiled too. The flames of the bonfire projected our shade toward the surroundings making them darker.

— What was it like to be in the tunnel of the inner secrets? —I was asked by one of the old men, without knowing whom of them or why he knew it.
— I travelled by it more calmly and realized the warmth of the place; I could see myself as I was this morning, writing in my study, before escaping of myself —I answered.

In the semidarkness, behind each one of the groups, somebody's silhouette was hardly distinguished, like making guard. Again, from the old men's group it was heard somebody said: "Go ahead!" Immediately, the one who was behind them went toward the hollow placed in front of the robust trunk of oak. For his elegant outfit and distinguished appearance, he could be a native or oriental hero. He neared the hollow and took a jícara, went toward the main maguey on the left side and from the hurt heart of the plant he filled the recipient with aguamiel, tear in cluster of the agave. He returned toward the holder, he placed himself standing inside it and looking toward us he held the bowl on high with his hands and emptied the content on his head.

— Look at how it disintegrates and becomes light! —Tao said.
— Just as it happened to us when we lost the lively memory —Huitzil added.

When the hero's sparkles got integrated to the maguey juice that was stored in the fountain, the three old men approached the place and drank it until drain it. After that, each one went back to their seat.

— Now you, Aralia —the oldest woman said.
— Yes! —the silhouette answered very sure.
— It is Voz! —we exclaimed, amazed that she could also hear and speak there.

Her shape was that of a princess of unhurried walking, wearing in the style of ceremonial Greek clothes, with a motif decorated white tunic with frets. She went to the same place as the hero and repeated the same actions, but she drank the juice of the main maguey that was at the right side. She was disintegrated too and the brightness of her body incorporated to the aguamiel. The three women, approaching the hollow, drank the liquid enriched with the princess' light and returned to their places.

Without noticing any previous indication, the guard who was behind us went to the oak with the decision and strength of a noble warrior. Without any hesitations, he carried out the ceremony and offered firmly the light of his admirable shape to the aguamiel.

> — I guess it is our turn —Tao said, as the old men nodded their approval.
> — Let us drink that maguey juice —I invited them; and later we returned to our seats.

The aguamiel that contained the warrior's virtues produced us well-being and strength, but our bewilderment persisted.

> — What has happened? —we asked them.
> — It is the first stage of the integration ceremony —the old Sun answered.
> — But what does it consist of?
> — We nurture ourselves from our guards' memory of experiences.
> — What for?
> — To have the necessary confidence in the ceremony of the third road, something that they perfectly know.
> — Without any reserve, they bequeathed us their teachings, is it right?
> — They have done the same thing, not any other —they concluded—. Do you want to go on?

Tao, Huitzil and I hesitated, contrary to the women who accepted to follow.

The unexpected happenings caused that the bonfire, liven up by restless, made our shades bigger and impelled them every time with more strength toward the cosmos, invading its constellations.

> — Since we are here, let us going ahead —Huitzil said.

Without hesitating, Cometa was incorporated and proceeded to do what our guards had done, and his enlightened body was crumbled until the juice of maguey received the legacy of his outstanding knowledge of the cosmos.

Yauh: The inner exit

Pacindo and the old man from the ship went to drink the maguey juice and drop after drop assimilated that distilled of wisdom.

Later it was the turn of the old Sun to perform the rite, although before doing it he said goodbye to Pacindo and told him: "In the union of the matter equality is found"; and he emptied the aguamiel on the high part of his body until he fused together with the liquid. Pacindo drank that flow of experiences with a special respect and went back to his seat. By that time, his body irradiated a wise brightness.

— Who will be the next one now? —Huitzil asked.

Desamor went toward the hollow to perform the ceremony, until her light formed part of the refulgent liquid that, in spite of its coldness, was drunk by the other two women.

Later the most mature woman went with decision toward the beautiful tree in order to practise the ritual. She did it twice with the maguey juice from the right side and nothing happened. She went toward the left side agave and remained.

— What will happen with the three of us? —Huitzil asked alarmed.
— I cannot imagine —Tao answered.

Pacindo had to fulfil the same rite without any effects on his memory of experiences. He did it twice with aguamiel of the left side and once with the liquid of the main agave at the right side, and his body instead of becoming transparent, acquired more brightness.

— Luna is the next —I told them.
— It is the most probably —they answered.

Moon was speaking to the mature woman and transmitting the following message: "Everything is the same, but different". She went toward the receptacle where her brilliant disintegration was accompanied by the gradual collapse of the full moon. From the celestial vault, like cry from the cosmos, rain like light was falling, similar to the one of fireflies of the sun we visited, it went extinguishing as the last woman finished drinking the most sublime maguey elixir. Already at her seat, addressing to me, we heard an invitation: "Now it is your turn, my son".

— It is Tlilal, your mother! —Tao exclaimed.
— Yes, it is she! —Huitzil said.

I got closer to hug her and kissed her, understanding the decision and courage with which she left me to the care of the river.

> — Who will go first? —I asked my friends.
> — Me! —the faithful Huitzil said determined, saying goodbye to us.

He supposed, as it happened, that he would be diluted in the maguey juice and did it firmly and as by enchant; Tao and I drank from its volatile water light with affection and gratitude. We promised ourselves always to remember it with joyfulness. Our bodies were more agile than ever.

> — I am the next one, Tao.
> — If you want me, I can go before you —he told me.

I thanked him his willingness, but I preferred to approach the oak and took a bath with aguamiel without suffering any change. I repeated the experience twice more and nothing happened. Leaning on the trunk of the oak there was Pacindo's striped walking stick and in its handle there was the mark of his right hand, a mark in the shape of a Y. "Pacindo, the calm and quiet Pacindo is my father", I thought, so many times together with him without knowing it. "My father, I have found my father at last", I shouted in my inner self.

> — That is right, Yauh, he is your father —Tlilal said without me asking her.

Tao, with the strength and dignity that characterized him, fulfilled the ritual. From his liberated body the most vivid brightness emanated, becoming one with the aguamiel. I drank its impetuous memory of experiences in its clear water light. I did it slowly, recalling what I learned from my friends and what I had shared with them.

Thoughtful, we remained in our places missing the ones that had become transparent.

The three of us approached the bonfire; we joined our intense light and our revitalized shadow.

> — Why have they left? —I asked them.
> — They have not left —my father responded—, they are within us.
> — Within us?
> — They have always been a part of each one of us, they are a reflection of ourselves —Tlilal said.
> — Remember that: "Everything is the same, but different" —Pacindo added.

— This has been our festivity —my mother said.
— Do they have theirs?
— That is how it is.

From what she said, I thought that, like in the multiple images of the parallel mirrors, there were as many ceremonies as there were participants in ours. In one of them Tao did not disappear and in another one Huitzil was entire.

— Your words call me down —I told them.
— You are in the space that correspond you.
— Is this my place?
— Our place.
— And what about if I were in another one?
— The same way they presented the flashes of their memory of experiences in order to enrich and strengthen our experiences and our encounter; you would do the same for them if you were in their cosmic space.
— What made me not see the third way on the previous occasions?
— It is visible only for the one who has succeeded in walking for the path of his own origin and went all over his own experiences. This allows you to have access to the fan of time and in a look understand humankind's history.
— Do they know other paths?
— Light goes and diffuses. In the same way, you went through certain roads and in the spaces that met you; you diffused your light; the options are limitless.
— This time we knew two roads.
— A new visit would take you to new directions, with such unexpected experiences as the ones you had this time: the difference is within you.
— What influenced so that we had certain experiences and not any others?
— The intensity of your unsatisfied wishes and the hidden secrets in your spirit.
— I would like there had been something like the road of the roads.
— It is the Great Road.
— Does it exist?
— Yes. It is found beyond the speed of light.
— Beyond the speed of light?
— Yes! Why not?
— Where does it take you?
— That speed would throw you to the dimension without dimensions.
— Which one is that one?
— The eternity... The absolute... The absolute eternity...

As we chatted, the bonfire continued increasing my parents' shade, as well as mine, projecting them toward the starry firmament. Our shades fused with the eternal night of the Universe. I remained deep in thought, while we drank water-light, light of water, light of light; and our shade grown, grown...

The lantern of reflection and feeling remained lighted on forever... We looked at each other. They were looks of meeting again, of integration, of unpractised love. Like shamans-gods, like mestizas-deities, their figures looked thrown to the space in their shade and everything was included that way.

We drank water-light in silence and devoutly, we drank until the absorbent night made us disappear.

Milton Keynes UK
Ingram Content Group UK Ltd.
UKHW030019180324
439604UK00001B/246